For Animals for Adoption in Accord, NY,

where we found Pico, our own rescue.

Dial Books for Young Readers
Penguin Young Readers Group
An imprint of Penguin Random House LLC
375 Hudson Street
New York, NY 10014

Text copyright © 2018 by Jacky Davis
Illustrations copyright © 2018 by David Soman

Printed in China
ISBN 9780399186400

10 9 8 7 6 5 4 3 2

Design by Jasmin Rubero
Text set in Old Claude

The art was created in ink and watercolor.

Ladybug
Girl
and the
Rescue Dogs

by David Soman and
Jacky Davis

Dial Books for Young Readers

"Wow, Bingo!" Lulu says as she flies around the
farmers' market, pointing to the colorful fruits and vegetables.
"It looks like a rainbow!"

Lulu and her mama are picking out peaches,
but Lulu stops when she notices
a big group of dogs under a banner.

They walk over to the table, and Lulu says, "Excuse me, please, who do these dogs belong to?"

"They're rescue dogs," replies the volunteer. "We're here to help them get adopted into good forever homes."

Lulu cannot believe these dogs have no homes!

She stands up very tall and says,

"I will rescue you!
I am Ladybug Girl!"

"Can we bring the dogs home?"
she asks her mama.

"Oh, Lulu, I really wish we could," Mama says. "But we already have Bingo.
And one dog is the right amount for our family."

Lulu wonders how Bingo would feel about having **eight dogs** crowded into their house.

It might be a bit much.

"Bingo, what are we going to do?
I can't rescue all the dogs myself, and Ladybug Girl
is supposed to save the day."

The volunteers from the shelter are busy caring for the dogs—
that's when Lulu notices that one of the water bowls is almost empty.
She realizes there *is* something Ladybug Girl can do to help!

Running over to the volunteer, she asks,
"Can I bring the dogs some water?"

"Yes, please!" says the busy woman,
handing her a pitcher.

Lulu rushes back with the water and carefully pours it into the bowl. The dogs happily guzzle it up.

As she turns to get more,

Lulu almost walks right into her Bug Squad friends.

"What are you doing?" asks Finny.

"I'm helping these dogs who need homes.

Want to help too?" asks Lulu.

"Yes!" answers Finny. "Definitely!"

"Let's find out what we can do," says Sam.

The woman from the shelter introduces them to the dogs.
"This is **Pico**,

Elvis,

Carter,

Otis,

Sassafras,

Daisy,

Ruby,

and Olive!"

she says.

"Each one needs to be brushed, played with, and given water and food.

Oh yes, they also *love* treats."

The Bug Squad listens carefully.

They understand how important all the little things are

in taking care of these dogs.

This might be their most important mission ever!

Bumblebee Boy fills Pico's bowl.

Pico is a very messy drinker.

He finds out that **Elvis** really loves his toy squid!

While **Sassafras** just wants to be scratched,

and scratched,

and scratched!

Grasshopper Girl plays catch with **Daisy** and **Otis**.
Daisy is extra bouncy, and can catch balls high in the air.

Otis needs . . . a little more practice.

She discovers that Carter will sit like a bunny—

if it means getting more treats!

Ladybug Girl sees that Ruby
really loves being brushed.

She keeps nudging closer
and closer until she is . . .

sitting in
Ladybug Girl's lap!

And **Olive** just wants to rest on her pillow.

"These dogs are so fun to be with," says Finny.

"Why hasn't anyone come to adopt them?"

"Maybe it's hard for people to see them over here," Sam says.

Lulu realizes Sam is right; everyone is too far away from the dogs.

She thinks for a moment, and then has an idea.

"What if we bring the *dogs* to *them*?" she asks Finny and Sam.

"This is a job for Ladybug Girl!"

"And Grasshopper Girl!"

"And Bumblebee Boy!"

They share their plan, and everyone quickly gets ready.
"Let the Pet Parade begin!" yells the Bug Squad!

They walk the dogs through the farmers' market,
carrying the banner high so everyone
will know that the dogs need homes.

People clap and cheer—and some even join in with their own pets!

The parade makes a circle around the market

and ends back where it began in the shade of the trees.

A family comes over.

"We're looking for a **big dog**," says the girl.

"But," adds her sister, "I want a dog that can sit in my lap."

"I know the perfect dog!" says Ladybug Girl.
"This is Ruby. Even though she's a big dog,
she also likes to sit in laps."

Before they know it, Ruby is sitting in *both* girls' laps.

"Do we have a dog?" asks their father.

"It looks like we do!" says their mother, and she goes to arrange the adoption.

"We did it!" Bumblebee Boy says. "We found Ruby a home."

"Let's come back next week and rescue other dogs," says Grasshopper Girl.

"All our help really mattered," adds Ladybug Girl.

"The Bug Squad saved the day!"